**Adapted by
David Lewman**

Random House 🏠 New York

© 2018 Viacom International Inc. and Viacom Overseas Holdings C.V.
All rights reserved. Published in the United States by Random House
Children's Books, a division of Penguin Random House LLC,
1745 Broadway, New York, NY 10019, and in Canada by
Penguin Random House Canada Limited, Toronto. Random House and
the colophon are registered trademarks of Penguin Random House LLC.
Nickelodeon, Rise of the Teenage Mutant Ninja Turtles, and all related titles,
logos, and characters are trademarks of Viacom International Inc. and
Viacom Overseas Holdings C.V.
Based on characters created by Peter Laird and Kevin Eastman.
rhcbooks.com
ISBN 978-0-525-64504-7 (trade)—ISBN 978-0-525-70766-0 (lib. bdg.)
Printed in the United States of America
10 9 8 7 6 5 4 3 2 1

CONTENTS

MASCOT MELEE

CHAPTER ONE

Hey, it's Raph! As the biggest, oldest, best-looking Turtle brother, I'm the leader. That just makes good sense. But even though I'm supposed to be in charge, my brothers manage to talk me into doing a lot of stuff I'm not all that psyched to do. Like the time I had to dress up as a mascot. You know, those costumed characters you see jumping around at sports events and hanging around Times Square in New York.

Sometimes they're big goofy dinosaurs or wacky pirates. Sometimes they're characters from your favorite movie or television show.

Anyway, here's what happened ...

Oh, wait. There's gonna be times in this story when you're gonna go, "Hey! How could he possibly know that? He wasn't there for that part!" Okay, I hear you. But the answer is my brothers told me all the parts I wasn't there for so I could tell you the whole deal.

Make sense?

Great! Let's go!

I was hot. I was sweaty. I couldn't see very well. But for once, I was out in the world, walking the streets of New York City instead of hiding in the sewer tunnels!

Usually we don't let people see us, because they tend to freak out when they notice four big walking, talking mutant Turtles. But this time, I was in disguise.

Still, I was nervous. What if something went wrong? Like it does pretty much every time we put one of Donnie's ideas into action...

I spoke into the microphone inside my headpiece. "What's the word? Am I clear?"

My three brothers could hear me through a speaker on the dashboard of our Turtle Tank.

"Looks *bueno* from here," Leo assured me, looking out the tank's dark-tinted windshield. I could hear him through my earpiece. He continued, "You are a go for Operation Let's Hope Raph Comes Back Alive."

"Will you stop calling it that?" I growled.

I was nervous enough about the operation without Leo giving it such a downer name.

"This is our first-ever exploratory expedition!" Donnie said, sounding a lot more positive than Leo. "They'll name sewers after you, Raph! I'd request the Third Street sewer. By far the best."

At this point, you probably want to know what my disguise was. Well, I guess I have to tell you. It was a hippo suit. That's right, a hippo. See, Donnie figured I'd fit right in with all the other costumed guys in Times Square. The plan made sense, but I have to admit, I didn't want to blend in too much. It would be nice if someone wanted to take my picture. I mean, my suit wasn't that bad.

So I made my way through the crowds of people, heading for this joint called Russ's Short, Hairy & Surly Clothing Store. I was on a mission.

"Go get Splinter's birthday gift!" Mikey said, cheering me on. "Our eyes depend on it!"

I remembered the moment that started this whole operation. The four of us were in our underground lair, watching TV. Our dad, Splinter, had come in wearing this ratty old robe. (Yeah, I know he's a rat, but that doesn't mean his clothes have to be ratty.)

"Oh, man!" I cried when I saw him in that robe.

"Cover up!" Leo begged.

"My eyes!" Mikey wailed.

"That mole is growing a mole," Donnie observed, disgusted. The robe revealed all kinds of stuff we had no interest in seeing.

Splinter ignored our comments. "Who's up for jumping jacks?"

He started doing jumping jacks, showing

us EVEN MORE stuff we didn't want to see! We freaked and shrieked!

"We gotta get him a new robe," Leo said.

And that's how I found myself shopping for a robe in Times Square, wearing a hippo costume.

CHAPTER TWO

Donnie flew a little drone with a camera over me so they could see where I was. Then they gave me directions to the store through my earpiece.

"Steady as she goes," Leo said, watching the video monitor in the Turtle Tank. "Old man on your right. Kid on your left. He's got peanut butter ice cream—"

"Your peanut allergies!" Donnie cried. "Evasive maneuvers!"

I made a hard right turn away from the kid with the ice cream. "Close one!" I said. "Man, this is crazy cool! First time any of us has moved through a crowd totally unnoticed!"

"The hippo suit is great," Mikey agreed, "but I still think trench coats would've worked."

"We could barely save up enough for one robe," Leo reminded him. "How could we possibly afford four trench coats?"

At that moment "video text from April" appeared on the dashboard monitor in the Turtle Tank. Donnie clicked away from the live drone feed to look at the video. It showed a little animated hippo with a turtle head, flying through the sky, leaving a trail of cookies behind it.

"April's memes are so lit!" Mikey said.

"I know you think I wouldn't like cookies

coming out of butts," Donnie said, "but I do."

When he clicked back to the live feed, he saw a bearded dude bump into me and grab onto me to keep from falling down.

"Sorry, my bad," I said, even though it wasn't.

The dude with the beard nodded and walked on. I took a couple more steps and found I was standing right in front of the clothing store. I reached into my pocket for my wallet and found ... nothing!

"My wallet?" I whispered so my brothers couldn't hear. "My wallet!"

I turned to the nearest tourist. "Have you seen my wallet?" I asked frantically. "There's a skull on it. And a Teddy Bear Town frequent buyer card inside."

The tourist shook his head. I ran to the next tourist.

In the Turtle Tank, Donnie asked Leo,

"Did Raph say he lost his wallet?"

"Raph!" Leo yelled into the mic. "Did you lose our money?"

"No," I lied to them. Then I whispered to the tourist, "Have you seen my lost money?"

"You DID lose it!" Donnie cried.

I whipped around to ask more tourists if they'd seen my money, but I slammed into this big dude, and my HIPPO HEAD CAME OFF! EVERYONE COULD SEE ME!

CHAPTER THREE

I gasped. My brothers gasped. And the tourists gasped.

All staring at me.

I was sure I was sunk. They'd haul me off and throw me in a lab for scientists to experiment on, and I'd never be seen again.

A woman with a baby walked up to me. Here it came . . . the scream. The call for the police . . .

But then . . . she smiled! "Your costume!

It's great! You're the Turtle-Potamus meme, right?"

"What meme?" I asked. "I mean ... yes, *that* meme. Which meme, now?"

She pointed up to the huge video screen hanging over Times Square. On it was the same flying hippo with a turtle head meme that April had sent us.

"Yes!" I agreed. "I'm *that*! There's nothing else I could possibly be." I breathed a huge sigh of relief, and so did my brothers.

"You're the best—and cleanest—Times Square mascot I've ever seen! Here's my baby. He loves memes."

She shoved her baby into my hands and took our picture with her phone. Then she took back her baby and crammed money into my hands.

"Uh, ma'am?" I said. "You've misplaced your five-dollar bill directly into my hand."

"Roll with it, bud," Leo said in my ear. "She's paying you for the picture. Keep working the crowd and maybe you can get back our money you lost."

"*Allegedly* lost," I corrected him.

Before I knew it, all these tourists were posing with me and dropping money into my hippo head! "Hear ye, hear ye, people of Times Square!" I called, getting into it. "The most famous Turtle-Hippo in the world is available for pictures and *quinceañeras*!"

"This is so great!" Mikey said in the Turtle Tank.

"Yeah," Donnie said, "but look at those four mascots standing together. They don't look real happy about Raph's success."

There were four mascots glaring at me. One was a superhero bird with a pointy beak named Sergeant Woodpecker. Next to him was a superheroine with a full mask and a hammer who called herself Atomic Lass. The third was a dog with a metal chain called Joey the Junkyard Puppy. And the fourth mascot was a robot vampire. I think she was called Robot Vampire.

"*Nobody* takes tourists away from Atomic Lass!" growled the superheroine with the hammer.

She and the other three mascots headed straight toward me. . . .

CHAPTER FOUR

The angry mascots nudged tourists away and formed a circle around me.

Everyone watched, waiting to see what would happen next. A few people whipped out their phones and started snapping pictures.

Atomic Lass shouted to the crowd, "I can't believe you guys are falling for this hack! Memes come and go, but we classic characters have always been here for you! For a small fee."

Sergeant Woodpecker pecked at me with his pointy beak.

"Hey!" I protested. "That's not very neighborly!"

"Show this buttinski how we mascot downtown, Robot Vampire!" Sergeant Woodpecker yelled.

Robot Vampire started singing and unleashed a high kick that caught me right in the chest. *"If you wanna make friends, you gotta know your place!"*

"Easy there, hoss," I warned.

Joey the Junkyard Puppy joined her, snapping his chain in my face. *"Don't step on people's paws, or they'll get in your face!"*

"I'm just saying you don't wanna mess with me," I said.

Atomic Lass sang, *"If you do what we tell you, then you're gonna be fine,"* as she bashed my knee with her hammer. It hurt, but I tried to keep my cool. Then she stole my hippo head and tossed it to Robot Vampire.

"Now, that crosses a line," I said.

Sergeant Woodpecker danced over, singing, *"Or else there'll be an oopsie, and I'll break your spine!"* He elbowed me, sending me falling backward over Joey the Junkyard Puppy, who'd crouched down behind me.

A few tourists clapped half-heartedly, unsure how to respond to this act.

In the Turtle Tank, my brothers saw the other mascots bullying me. "No way!" Leo said. "Nobody punks Raph like that. Except for us. Suit up!"

Seconds later, the doors of the Turtle Tank flew open, revealing Mikey, Leo, and Donnie dressed as Turtle Aliens from our favorite television show, *Jupiter Jim*. Donnie wore antennae made out of coat hangers. Mikey had on a fishbowl space helmet.

Leo was just himself. Then he clipped on a fanny pack.

"Time to teach those jerks a lesson!" Leo said. "And earn back that money for Pop's gift! *Jupiter Jim* Turtle Aliens ahoy!"

"Yeah!" Mikey said.

"Right!" Donnie agreed.

They leapt away from the tank and sprang through the air with ninja ease. Even in their makeshift costumes, they looked awesome as they sailed past the flashing lights of Times Square.

Meanwhile, the four mascots were still hassling me. Robot Vampire stuck my hippo head in tourists' faces. How were they doing this to me, the toughest mutant in town? I knew this situation had to change!

"Remember to tip Robot Vampire or she'll suck your blood," Sergeant Woodpecker told the crowd. Then he turned to me and snarled, "And we'll spill yours if you ever invade our turf again, ya puke!"

But right at that moment, Donnie, Leo, and Mikey flipped over the tourists' heads, landing right in the four mascots' dance zone!

"*Jupiter Jim*'s Turtle Aliens flying in to rescue one of their own!" Leo announced to the crowd.

For a second, the whole city seemed to freeze. I swear the traffic was even silent. The mascots and the onlookers didn't know what to make of these new characters.

Then suddenly, everyone cheered. The tourists LOVED this show.

CHAPTER FIVE

"I can't believe I'm this close to my childhood idol, Atomic Lass!" Donnie exclaimed. We glared at him. "Oh, right," he said. "Bad guys."

Sergeant Woodpecker growled, "Show these folks how we mascot downtown, Robot Vampire!"

We got ready to fight.

The mascots jumped into position.

Robot Vampire rolled toward us, flung open her cape, and . . .

. . . hit the button on a boom box.

Thump. Thump. Thump.

Music pulsed from the speakers, and she started to dance.

Joey the Junkyard Puppy leapt in and did an impressive spin move.

People cheered. A passing taxi honked approvingly. I saw what was going on—these characters were challenging us to a dance off. I turned to our beats expert. All I had to say was "Mikey?"

He knew just what I meant. Mikey turned to Donnie and said, "Donnie?"

Donnie was on it. He said, "Activate music mode!" A stereo with turntables flew up out of his battle shell and landed right in front of Mikey, who got to work doing his DJ bit, spinning and scratching on the turntables.

Leo vaulted into the circle the mascots were dancing in. Wielding his *odachi* sword, he faced off with Joey the Junkyard Puppy.

"Time to go to obedience school!"

"No fair," Joey protested. "Bringing a sword to a chain fight!" He whipped his long chain at Leo, but Leo kept dodging and moving closer until . . . *BAM!* He knocked Joey down! "Now who's a bad boy?" he crowed. "That's right—YOU are!"

"OOOOOOOH!" and "AAAAAH!" the tourists gasped, thinking this was all part of a well-rehearsed routine.

Atomic Lass threw some dance moves at Leo, but Donnie swept in on his rocket-powered *tech-bo*. "Out of the way!" he shouted. "*I* get to dance with her!"

He showed her all his best moves, ending in a dip. "Any chance you and Atomic Lad are splitsville?" he asked eagerly.

WHAM!

Sergeant Woodpecker knocked Donnie away with a flying kick. Still dancing, the mascot gloated. "You dance as good as you cosplay, boy!"

I squared off with Sergeant Woodpecker. "Hey! Dance-pick on somebody your own size!" I gave him all my best dance moves, which were pretty sweet, if I do say so myself.

But Atomic Lass and her two pals countered with some amazing break dancing, ending with a challenging pose. "Bring it, ya pukes!" Sergeant Woodpecker bellowed.

Mikey slammed a smoke bomb onto the pavement.

POOF!

We vanished in a thick purple cloud and reappeared on a ledge high above the crowd. At that exact moment, Donnie made the Turtle-Potamus meme appear on screens all around Times Square. And we went into an amazing dance routine, moving in perfect unison.

"Oh, it has been broughten!" I announced. "Now let's go get Dad's robe!"

Furious, Atomic Lass hurled her hammer at us! We ducked, and the hammer slammed into a wall behind us.

Lunging forward, Atomic Lass grabbed Donnie's *tech-bo* staff. The two of them struggled for control of it. Atomic Lass pressed a button on the staff, and it changed into a rocket! Donnie shook her off, but the staff shot out of his hands, fired into Atomic Lass and . . .

. . . KNOCKED HER HEAD OFF!

"Oh no!" Donnie cried. "No, no!"

"Omigosh!" Mikey cried. "You knocked that lady's top clean off!"

But her body jumped to its feet, and out of the costume's neck hole popped the head of . . .

. . . THE DUDE WITH THE BEARD WHO'D BUMPED INTO ME!

"You!" I said. Behind us, a latch on the hammer popped open, and wallets and jewelry spilled out! The crowd gasped! I spotted my skull wallet. "You stole my wallet!" I shouted. "It better still have my Teddy Bear Town card in it!"

But as I reached for my wallet, Sergeant Woodpecker tried to knock my head off with his long, sharp beak.

"Let's see what YOUR ugly mug looks like!" he yelled.

BAM!

I punched the mascot, and his mask popped off, too!

He stood up, and the rest of us stared, waiting to see who would emerge from his costume's neck hole. But when his face came out, he was . . . A MUTANT COCKROACH!

"GAAAH!" we screamed.

The other two mascots pulled off their heads, revealing that they were mutant cockroaches, too! Even the bearded guy pulled off a disguise, revealing the cockroach head underneath.

"Metamorphosis! That took an unexpected left turn," Donnie observed.

CHAPTER SIX

The crowd gasped, screamed, and ran for their lives.

"You thought you were the only mutants in New York?" the former Sergeant Woodpecker snarled.

I stepped up to him. "Look, all we wanted was a little money to buy our pops a gift!"

"Boo hoo!" he said sarcastically, holding up my Teddy Bear Town card. "Tell it to one of your teddy bears!" Then the evil mutant cockroach RIPPED MY CARD TO SHREDS!

That did it.

"Don't you DARE make fun of Dr. Huggenstein or Mr. Cuddles!" I roared. Then I wound up and clobbered him with everything I had. As the mutant went flying, my brothers jumped in.

But the mutant cockroaches weren't going down without a fight, and they were tough! They sent Leo flying into a food cart, but he squirted mustard in their eyes.

As the Atomic Lass cockroach tried to smash Donnie with her hammer, he hit a button on his wrist com and called out, "Spider shell, engage!"

The metallic shell auto-launched from the Turtle Tank, flew through the air, and latched onto Donnie's back.

"Let's get everybody their money back!" Donnie shouted. With the press of a button, he extended four robotic arms from the mechanical shell. But the mutant cockroach countered with her SIX legs!

Meanwhile, Mikey used his *kusari-fundo* to snare the Robot Vampire cockroach, swing her around, and fling her across Times Square. "You give Robot Vampire cockroaches a bad name!" he yelled.

Donnie was still fighting the Atomic Lass cockroach. "You're ruining my childhood fantasy of the two of us fighting crime together in Uraniumville," he complained.

She bit his *tech-bo* staff with her razor-sharp mandibles. "You leave me no choice," Donnie said sadly. "But we'll always have Times Square." He pressed a button on the staff. Energy surged through it, blasting the mutant into a trash bin.

The Joey the Junkyard Puppy cockroach tried to run off with our hippo head full of dough, but I stopped him with a well-placed punch. *SOCK!* I caught the hippo head, with all our money, and held it up high. "Boom! Thank you, Times Square!"

Back in our underground lair, Splinter was still wearing his crummy old robe. He opened the box from Russ's Clothing Store and held up the luxurious new silk robe we'd gotten him.

"My sons, you honor me!" he exclaimed. "The silky smoothness against my fur— unparalleled. It's really exquisite." He folded the robe and put it back in the box. "I will save it for only the most special occasions."

"What?!" we all exclaimed.

"Now," Splinter went on, "who's up for training? As luck would have it, I'm already wearing my jumping jacks robe!"

Splinter started doing jumping jacks, and we all looked away in horror. Who knew a bunch of mutant cockroaches wouldn't be the scariest thing we'd see that day?

DOWN WITH THE SICKNESS

CHAPTER ONE

"**A**re you ready for a STORY? Told to you by MIKEY? I THOUGHT SO! THEN HERE WE GO! LISTEN UP!

We were in our lair's arcade, watching Raph play an electronic dance game. Wait, did you know that we have our own arcade in the lair? It's awesome! If you're ever in the lair looking for me, check the arcade first. That's always your best bet for finding me.

Anyway, Raph was doing great. His big feet were on the move, stepping and crossing! He ran! He jumped! He spun! Raph was ROLLING UP THE SCORE!

"I don't think he's got this," Leo said.

I told Leo to leave him alone.

"What?" Leo asked. "I'm just saying he doesn't have this! Just my opinion! It's a free country, ain't it?"

Raph nudged Leo away from the dance game. "You're just trying to get inside my head so I don't top your score, is what you're doing."

"Oh my peaches and cream, he just doubled!" Donnie noted.

Nearby, I thought I faintly heard something being dragged across the floor. But I ignored the sound. I was too caught up in the excitement of Raph's great game.

"Rag!" Raph ordered.

I quickly grabbed a rag and wiped sweat off his brow. "Have I ever told you how big and beautiful you are?"

"No," Raph growled. "And thank you."

Donnie was practically jumping up and down with excitement. "He's about to set a new high score!"

That meant beating Leo's high score, which is all we cared about. If we weren't all so busy watching this incredible moment, we would have heard the thing sneaking up behind us.

If we'd been listening, we'd have heard its limping steps getting closer and closer.

CRASH!

It sounded like somebody was knocking over glasses. But we ignored that, too.

Suddenly, we heard a terrible moan

behind us.

"BRAAAAIINNNN!"

It was Splinter's voice.

Raph stopped dancing as we all turned to look at the arcade's doorway. We stood frozen with surprise. Our eyes were wide. Our mouths hung open.

"Game over," announced the dance game.

Splinter was standing there with his eyes rolling in their sockets, looking like a zombie! "Oh," he groaned. "My braaaaain!"

"YAAAAAAHHH!" we all screamed.

Splinter sneezed a cute little sneeze. "Achoo!"

"Gesundheit," Leo said.

"Omigosh, omigosh, omigosh!" I cried. "Splinter's a ZOMBIE!"

But Donnie quickly corrected me. (Correcting me seems to be one of his favorite things.) "Mikey, zombies are interested in *other* people's brains."

"Rat Flu!" Raph announced. "This is not a drill. I repeat, this is *not* a drill, boys."

We set up a tent around Splinter. Inside, we hovered over him as he lay on the floor.

"I feel terrible," he groaned. "Do I look terrible? Be honest!"

POP! A snot bubble burst by his nose. We all screamed and jumped back. I landed on Raph's back.

"You look great!" Raph lied. "Not horribly sick at all!"

We hurried out of the sick tent.

"He's horribly sick," Raph whispered once we were out of there.

"Look, a flu this intense is going to affect

all areas of his brain," Donnie lectured. "I'm talking the full seven stages before his body naturally heals itself." The full seven stages! That was bad.

Real bad.

CHAPTER TWO

"**Y**ou guys know what the full seven stages mean," Raph said seriously, putting his arms around me and Leo. He brightened. "Another chance to get WHATEVER WE WANT!"

We all got excited. Raph was right! Once Splinter reached stage seven, he'd give us anything we asked for! That was how Rat Flu worked! Whoever caught it went through seven bizarro stages. And in the last stage, the sickie couldn't say no to any request! SO SWEET!

IF, that is ... we were healthy enough to ask him. We'd never managed to stay healthy before. Rat Flu is SUPER contagious.

Raph knew what were all thinking. "This year's gonna be different!" he declared. "No one's getting bit! No one's getting infected!"

"When we do make it to the end, which I'm now calling the Must Say Yes stage," Leo said, "what are we gonna ask for?"

Excellent question! We all thought hard. Then we turned to Raph.

"Well, uh," he stammered. "This year I was thinking we could ask for ... uh ... um ... er ..."

"Aw, he's got nothing!" Leo groaned. "We're dead!"

"Hey! I got something, all right?" Raph said. "Like a ... um ..."

"URANIUM!" Donnie interrupted. "We should ABSOLUTELY ask for uranium! If I could get my hands on a little of that, we'd be virtually unstoppable!"

But I had a better idea. "What about a brick oven for pizza?!"

Leo shoved me and Donnie aside. "Who's gonna CLEAN that? What we should ask for is matching uniform onesies! Those are SICK! Pun intended. And I nailed it."

The three of us started fighting over whose idea was best, but Raph stopped us. "Enough! I got this! I'm gonna ask Splinter for something that benefits ALL of us!"

"THIS IS SO EXCITING!" I shouted. "But terrible for Dad." Then I noticed something: when I breathed out, I could see my breath!

Raph exhaled. We could all see his breath, too. "Buckle up, boys," he warned. "It's about to get weird."

In his room, Splinter had turned the air-conditioning all the way up. But he still felt hot, because he was in stage one of Rat Flu: FEVER!

He fanned himself. Then he picked up his electric razor. . . .

Hours later, out in the main room, we tried to keep warm. We had a heat lamp on, but we were still shivering. "I hate stage one," I said miserably. "Think warm thoughts: pizza ovens, bricks from Italy, wood chips roasting . . ."

"We're four hours in," Raph said. "His fever's gotta break soon."

Wearing a parka and sipping cocoa, Leo was feeling nice and cozy. "I told you guys to plan ahead," he gloated. "Now I'm sitting here all warm and toasty." He took another sip, but then looked up and spit it out. "Wha—wha—WHY?!"

Splinter stood in the doorway, shaved smooth. "Had to air myself out," he explained feverishly. He fell forward, landing facedown on the floor. But then he raised himself up and . . . GROWLED AT US!

He was entering . . . stage two: WILD RAT MAN!

Scampering on all fours and squeaking like a feral rat, Splinter chased us around the lair!

"Suits on! Suits on!" Raph barked. "Donnie, get the device ready!"

We quickly pulled on hazmat suits— plastic coveralls that are supposed to protect you from hazardous materials.

"Oh, the device is ready," Donnie said proudly. "My inspiration was simplicity. Why dress something up with lots of—"

"No one has time for this," Leo interrupted impatiently while being chased by Splinter.

Donnie rolled his eyes and pressed a button on his wristband. A giant hamster ball rolled into the room.

"Whoa," Raph said. "Nice! Let's get him inside."

Leo tossed a homemade pizza into the ball, and Splinter dove in after it. Donnie plugged the ball's opening. "This should hold him for a while," Donnie said.

"You sure this isn't cruel?" Leo asked.

Raph shook his head. "He *loves* pizza and confined spaces you can barely breathe in."

I watched as Splinter pushed against the inside of the ball to roll it around the room, slamming into walls. *WHAM!*

Donnie held on to the plug like the rope

on a bucking bronco. "Donnie," I asked, "is the ball going to hold up?"

"MOST DEFINITELYYYYYYY!" he called, riding the ball around the lair.

CRASH!

The ball shattered! Donnie hit the floor. Splinter scurried through a hole in the wall.

Uh-oh.

CHAPTER THREE

Raph beckoned me. "Mikey, follow me, and be careful. We can't afford to lose anyone before stage seven."

"I thought we all agreed it was now called the Must Say Yes stage!" Leo protested.

"It would be easier for me to be careful if I knew you were going to ask for a pizza oven," I suggested.

"I'm still thinking!" Raph answered.

"Quick question," Donnie said from the

floor. "Is uranium still on the table?"

Wearing our hazmat suits, Raph and I crept into Splinter's darkened bedroom shining a flashlight, looking for him.

"Where's Splinter?" I whispered. "Do you smell him?"

Raph crossed to the bed. He bent down, grabbed the comforter, and whipped it off.

A bug skittered out. Otherwise, nothing.

Actually, there was something, but Raph was looking in the wrong place. "Well, he's not under there," Raph said.

I stared at him, too terrified to tell him what I was seeing.

Raph could sense something was horribly wrong. "What? What's going on? Use your words."

"He's . . . on . . . you," I squeaked, terrified. *Splinter was on Raph's back!*

"Heats on stew?" Raph said, puzzled.

"He's . . . on . . . you," I whispered.

"He's on me?" Raph whispered, going pale.

"Yes," I whispered.

Raph slowly tilted the flashlight so it was shining up at himself. We gasped at what we saw—and heard!

SQUEAK! SQUEAK!

Splinter started making awful wild rat sounds.

"AAAAH!" Raph screamed, shaking him off. Splinter flew across the room and smacked into the wall.

He stood up, but instead of scurrying around the room like a wild rat, Splinter suddenly stretched out his arms for a hug. "Oh, my favorite son," he said.

"Favorite son?" I said. Then I realized what was happening. "RUN!"

We sprinted out of his room and into the

main room. Splinter followed us, walking with his arms out. "Stage three!" Raph called to Donnie and Leo. "Stage three!"

"Oh no," Donnie said. "Captain Cuddle Cakes."

Yes, Splinter had entered stage three of his Rat Flu: CAPTAIN CUDDLE CAKES! "I need hugs!" he exclaimed as he chased us.

Raph noticed Donnie and Leo had taken off their hazmat suits. "What're you doing outta your suits?!"

"It was Leo's idea," Donnie said, pointing at him.

"No one forced you, Donnie!" Leo countered. "Also, I was hot."

Splinter had almost reached them.

"Suits on!" Raph ordered. "Suits on!"

Leo and Donnie struggled to get back into their suits, running and zipping as fast as they could. Donnie got his on first, but

Leo had trouble working the zipper. *ZZZIP!* "Got it!"

Leo looked around, puzzled. "What's that smell?"

We heard Splinter say "I love you THIS much"...

...FROM INSIDE LEO'S SUIT!

CHAPTER FOUR

"**L**eo's down! Leo's down!" Raph shouted, meaning he'd been infected by Splinter's hug.

"We've got to quarantine him!" Donnie said.

"Sure," I said, "but first we've got to isolate him so he doesn't get us sick!"

"THAT'S WHAT 'QUARANTINE' MEANS!" Donnie yelled.

"Right," I said. "Totally knew that."

Within seconds, we had Leo in his room. Donnie sealed the doorway with a quarantine tarp. In the main room, Splinter hugged a martial arts training dummy.

"Hey, you need me to get to the Must Say Yes stage," Leo protested. "We need to ask for the onesies—" He paused, cocking his head. "Whoa, it is REALLY hot! Is there a fire? There's a fire here, right? The floor's made of lava?"

Stage one: Fever! Raph hit a button. *FWOOSH!* Nozzles blasted Leo with antibiotic spray.

"Down to three of us," Raph said. "All right, fellas, let's be careful so the rest of us can make sure we get to stage seven and get what we want." He looked around. "Who has eyes on the package?"

I pointed to the training dummy, now covered in slobbery kiss marks. Splinter was gone! "I lost him," I admitted.

POOF! A smoke bomb went off! We all coughed. When the smoke settled, we saw Splinter standing perfectly still, dressed all in black.

Like a ninja.

Carrying a *katana* sword, he ran straight at us, throwing *shuriken*—sharp, pointy little ninja stars. *FWIT! FWIT! FWIT!* Raph guarded his face with his *tonfa*. *THONK! THONK! THONK!* The stars stuck in his *tonfa*.

It was obvious to us that Splinter had reached stage four: NINJA SUPREME!

POOF! Another smoke bomb! This time, Splinter jumped through the smoke before it cleared. Yelling Lou Jitsu's catchphrase, "HOT SOUP," Splinter sliced off our hazmat suits with the *katana.* And then he vanished AGAIN!

"Where'd Splinter go?" Raph asked.

All the lights went out! Groping in the dark, I brushed against something. "Guys! I think I felt him!"

"Hey!" Donnie cried. "That's my butt!"

Raph dove through the darkness and tackled Donnie. "Ow! Would everyone please stop hitting me?"

Donnie lowered his goggles and switched them to night vision. But *I* still couldn't see! Thinking I'd found Splinter, I wrestled with him, yelling, "Now I've really got him! Take that, icky fuzz ball!"

It was Raph.

With his night vision goggles, Donnie spotted Splinter scurrying into his lab. "No, not my lab!" He cautiously followed Splinter. Raph and I waited, listening. We heard bangs and what sounded like Donnie crying out in pain.

ZWOOM! The lights came back on. Donnie

ran out of his lab with a small bandage on his arm, wiping sweat from his brow.

"Are you hit?" Raph asked.

"No, I'm fine," Donnie said. "I just cut myself on that janky old door. Did you decide what we're going to ask for?"

"Yeah!" Raph answered decisively. "I got it! I'm gonna ask for—"

But right then, Splinter dropped down by us, raised a microphone, and started to . . . SING!

CHAPTER FIVE

"I'M SO IN LOVE!" Splinter warbled. Which meant he'd definitely reached stage five: KARAOKE LOVE SONGS!

"I can't feel my ears!" I cried, trying to cover them. "Nothing is worth this!"

"We're so close," Raph said, even though he was clearly suffering. "Only two stages left!"

"And three totally healthy Turtles left," Donnie said in kind of a weird voice. We looked at him and couldn't believe what we saw. He was standing in a puddle of his own sweat! He was infected! "Man, why is it so hot in here?" he asked, just before passing out.

Raph and I zipped him into his room and blasted him with the antibiotic spray. He banged his fists against the plastic cover. "Oh, you're going to get squat from Splinter without Donnie!" he ranted. "I'm the brains behind this operation!" Then he sneezed a cute little sneeze. "Achoo!"

I turned to Raph. "Uh, what stage are we on now?"

CHAPTER SIX

Splinter set a *Jupiter Jim* action figure down on a stage. "Okay, we open in a noodle shop," he said, setting the scene. "It's raining!"

"Stage six!" Raph told me. "FAN FICTION!"

Splinter described an awesome battle between Jupiter Jim and some ninjas. "This is amazing!" I said, taking notes. "Keep going!"

"We're almost to stage seven!" Raph

enthused. "This is the closest I've been to success since . . . ever!" He started to high-five me. But just as our hands were about to touch . . .

. . . I sneezed! "Achoo!"

In what seemed like no time at all, I found myself in my room, sealed in just like Donnie and Leo! "We're done!" I wailed. "Raph is totally gonna blow this! He has no idea what to ask for! Which means— Hot! It's like I'm on the sun here!" *BWOOSH!* Raph blasted me with the antibiotic spray.

Chuckling triumphantly, Raph said, "I'm not gonna blow this."

"Raphael," Leo said in his sweetest voice, deep in the Captain Cuddle Cakes stage. "I love you, my brother, but you do tend to fail in big moments. But that's what makes you YOU. Now bring it in, buddy! I'm gonna hug you till a smile comes out!"

Leo tried to hug him through the protective tarp, but Raph knew the Captain Cuddle Cakes stage when he saw it. "Enough!" he snapped. "Raph's got this! In big-time moments, leaders make big-time shots! And I'm big-time!"

WHAM! Donnie slammed into the tarp, clearly in the Wild Rat Man stage. "Yesssss!" he hissed, drooling. "Make him say yesssssssss!"

"Enough!" Raph barked at us. "Don't mess this up, Raph," he said to himself, psyching himself up.

"Don't forget we only get to ask for one thing, my little Raphadoodle!" Leo crooned.

"I know exactly what I'm asking for," Raph said. He walked slowly toward Splinter, who was finally in stage seven! Raph stopped, staring. Father and son faced each other like two guys fighting a duel in the Old West.

"Master Splinter," Raph said seriously, choosing his words carefully. "I know you'll say yes to whatever I ask for. I want you to give—"

"RAPHADOODLE A HUG!" Leo shouted. He whipped out his sword, sliced through the containment plastic, and collapsed between Raph and Splinter. "Everybody loves hugs!"

"WHAT?!" Raph screamed. "No! Anything but that!"

Too late. Splinter ran, leapt through the air, and knocked Raph to the ground in a fierce, loving embrace.

"Achoo!" Raph sneezed adorably.

When he heard Raph sneeze, Splinter rubbed his hands together greedily. "Ooh, Rat Flu! I can't wait until stage seven. Papa wants a new bike!"

ORIGAMI
TSUNAMI

CHAPTER ONE

Pretty good job telling that story, Mikey. And yours was good, too, Raph. But now it's time to step aside, take a seat, and give a listen, 'cause Leo's here, and it's STORYTELLIN' TIME!

We were in the lair watching *Teriyaki Shakedown,* one of our all-time favorite movies, starring our very favorite action hero, LOU JITSU! We'd seen it so many times, we had all the lines and moves memorized.

In the movie, two mobsters threatened a cook in a noodle house. Standing in front of the screen, Donnie and Mikey pretended to be the mobsters, while Raph took the part of the cook, who was really Lou Jitsu, the martial arts expert! On the couch, Splinter tried to see around us.

One mobster said, "Where's our free grub, noodle man?"

"Okay," Lou Jitsu said. "How 'bout some . . . HOT SOUP?!"

He grabbed the bad guys' wrists and flipped them right into these big pots of scalding-hot soup!

Raph did the same move and flipped Donnie and Mikey into beanbag chairs.

"AAHHH!" the mobsters in the movie screamed.

"Too spicy for you?" Lou Jitsu asked. He shook his head. "Everyone's a critic."

Donnie jumped up out of the beanbag chair. "Man!" he said. "*Teriyaki Shakedown* always gets me so JAZZED!"

"Yeah," Raph agreed. "Lou Jitsu's the business!"

Splinter slowly stood up from the couch. "Then why do you insult the master with your poor technique? HOT SOUP!" He expertly flipped Mikey and Donnie across the room. "Don't worry," he said calmly, sitting back down. "Someday, with a little practice, you'll be great ninjas . . . is something I'd say if I were a liar."

Mikey didn't realize we'd just been insulted. "That's nice of you to say, Pop, but I'm tired of practicing."

"Yeah, we can be heroes like Lou Jitsu!" Raph said, punching the air.

Splinter laughed and said, "Nice try."

"We got the squillz," Mikey said. "We got the tight color-coordinated team look."

"Let's do it!" Raph said, pumped up by the movie. "Let's go out and bust some bad guys!"

Donnie nodded. "Yeah, I just feel like, you know, we need a case to get the juices flowing a little bit. Let's see what the internet has to say about it." He picked up a tablet and started searching for a mission.

That's when I came back into the room, chewing on a slice of pizza I'd snagged from the fridge.

"Yo, Leo!" Mikey called. "We're gonna be heroes!"

I plopped down in the beanbag chair, upside down. "Okay, what's the plan? Solve the city's rat problem?"

"Hey now!" Splinter objected, smacking me with his tail. "I am standing right here!"

Raph made a face. "No way! We're crime fighters!"

Donnie lifted the tablet for us to see. "Check this out! The Spine-Breaking Bandit!"

"Yeah!" Raph said, pumping a fist. "Go big or go home!"

I wasn't so sure we were ready for a super-dangerous job. Sometimes my brothers get a little ahead of themselves. "Yeah, go home on a STRETCHER. What else you got?"

Donnie flipped through more cases on his tablet. "Oh, here's a good one! The Long Island Mangler!"

"Okay, Donnie," I said. "I appreciate you giving your best effort, but maybe we should save mangling and spine-breaking for our

SECOND day?" I was hoping to convince them to tackle something a little more our speed.

"All right, well, this one's kind of lame," Donnie said, pausing on another option. "Someone stole paper from a delivery truck."

I hopped up out of the beanbag chair and applauded. "There it is! There you go! That's exactly the kind of junior-level mischief we can put an end to!"

CHAPTER TWO

"**R**eally?" Raph asked doubtfully. "That'll make us heroes? It's only paper."

I turned to him. "Only PAPER?! Oh, yeah, that's what they all say! You think the road to hero town is paved with real crime? No! It's paved with the tears of the poor paper man. And who helps that guy? I'll tell you who: *we* are who."

My brothers were silent for a second, then cheered, "YEAH!"

My little speech worked like a charm.

The four of us rushed out, ready to solve the stolen paper case. This would be a piece of cake!

It was night. We made our way across the city. Donnie flew in his quadcopter. We landed on a rooftop.

"What kind of weirdo steals paper?" Raph asked.

"A dreamer!" Mikey answered. "You look at a blank sheet and see nothing. They see possibilities!"

"There's only one store they haven't hit," Donnie said. "And it's right over there."

He pointed down to a store. A van was parked right in front, and two shadowy figures were loading paper into it.

"How 'bout we go stealth and make 'em wish they stole toilet paper?" Raph said.

That made us laugh.

We silently made our way down to the street, but the thieves must've heard us somehow, because they ran, one around each side of the building. Raph took charge: "Leo and Donnie, you two go left. Mikey, go right. I'll take the roof and swoop down like a boss!"

So Donnie and I headed along the left side of the building to the back while Mikey went right and Raph quickly climbed up to the roof.

But when Donnie and I rounded the corner, we smacked right into Mikey! "Oof!" he gasped. We looked around the parking lot, which was surrounded by high walls. "Whoa," Mikey said. "Where are they?"

Raph jumped down from the roof, yelling,

"SWOOPIN' LIKE A BOSS!" He was coming straight for us! He landed right on top of us! *WHOMP!*

SCREECH!

The van was taking off! We ran to the front of the store and got there in time to see the van speeding away!

CHAPTER THREE

We stared at the van as it disappeared around a corner. "Uh, quick question: Did we seriously just get schooled by paper thieves?" Donnie asked, bewildered.

Raph shook his head, disgusted with himself. "I don't swoop like a boss. I swoop like a noob."

"Man, this seemed like a really cool idea until we didn't succeed at it," Mikey said. All three of my brothers hung their heads, discouraged.

I could see that it was time for a little pep talk, Leo-style! "Whoa, whoa! Where'd my brothers go? Mikey, where's your legendary optimism? Raph, where's your go-getter attitude? Donnie, where's your . . . emotionless passion?"

"Here," Donnie said in a flat voice.

I paced around, slamming my fist into my palm. "We can still catch these lame old paper crooks and be heroes!"

"Yeah, that's gonna be hard," Donnie pointed out. "This was the last paper store in town."

"Hmm . . . ," I said, thinking. Then I got a brilliant idea and grinned. "Or *was* it?"

"Yeah, I literally just said that," Donnie said.

In a crummy part of the city, where it was easy to find an abandoned store, we quickly put together a fake paper shop. We hung a sign in the window: GRAND OPENING OF LEO'S PAPER HUT! (I won the fight over the name since the whole shebang was my idea.)

Our counter was made of cinder blocks. For a cash register, we had an old calculator duct-taped to a shoebox. For lighting, a flashlight hung from a rope. "It's beautiful!" Mikey enthused.

"You really think this fake shop'll hook the thieves?" Donnie asked skeptically. "The only paper we have is made from salami." He pointed to a stack of salami slices. I'd cut them myself with my *odachi* sword.

"Yes, it'll work," I assured him. "Raph,

stop eating the plan."

He stopped nibbling on a piece of salami and set it back on the stack. The bell by the front door rang. Our best friend, April O'Neil, came in with her resume.

"Hi, I'm here for the job interview," she said. Then she saw us. "Aw, no. I thought it was weird having a job interview at midnight."

Mikey whipped on reading glasses and checked his clipboard. "You are Miss . . . O'Neil, I believe?"

Just then, headlights shone through the front window. Someone was pulling up to the store!

CHAPTER FOUR

"**C**ustomers!" Mikey said, excited. "Okay, April, you're hired! Just follow the sales script and remember the customer is always right . . . unless he's a psychotic paper thief. We'll be in the back." He handed her the clipboard.

We piled into a cardboard box in the back labeled SECURITY BOOTH. It was a tight fit, but we all got in. Then we each tried to see through the peephole.

DING-A-LING! Someone was coming in the front door.

"Welcome to Leo's Paper Hut," we heard April say. "Can I interest you in our—MRFFF!"

"Mrfff?" Mikey whispered. "What's mrfff? She's supposed to say 'paper.'"

We heard struggling and someone ripping tape off a roll.

"Get outta the way!" Raph said, punching his fist through the cardboard. The box fell apart and we tumbled out onto the floor.

April was wrapped in duct tape and dangling from the ceiling by her waist, spinning slowly. A hankie had been stuffed in her mouth.

"April!" Raph cried.

"The salami paper!" Mikey said. "It's gone!"

Sure enough, the shelves were empty!

Outside, the van we'd seen at the real paper store peeled out.

April dropped to the floor. "Ow."

"No way!" I said as I watched the thieves drive off. "This was supposed to be easy! How do we keep losing these clowns?"

Donnie put his hand on my shoulder. "Leo, do you really think I would have let you make salami paper without putting a tracking device in it?"

He whipped out a handheld receiver. *BEEP!* The receiver showed that the signal was coming from ... Raph's stomach! Raph grinned sheepishly.

"It's okay," Donnie said. "I placed TWO tracking devices." He adjusted his receiver to find the other signal. "Got it! Let's go!"

We ran outside.

CHAPTER FIVE

Donnie's tracking thingy led us straight to the Brooklyn Navy Yard. Ducking down behind a stack of crates, we watched the thieves roll a cart loaded with paper up a ramp and into the cargo hold of a ship. I peered through binoculars.

"Okay, guys," I said softly. "This is our moment! They may have given us the slip before–"

"TWICE before," Mikey corrected me.

"Thank you, Mikey," I said. "Twice before. But now we've got them cornered, and there's nothing that can stop us!"

Stoked, we quickly made our way into the ship's cargo hold, where the two thieves were stacking reams of paper. They were dressed like ninjas, one small and one huge. Like, REALLY huge.

We snuck up on them.

"Okay, twerp and surprisingly big man," I said to them. "It's four against two, so what say we just call it a day?"

They turned around, and we got a better look at the two paper thieves. They were the weirdest-looking ninjas we'd ever seen!

"Whoa!" Mikey exclaimed. "They've got footprints tattooed on their faces!"

"Are those flames on their heads?" Raph asked. "They look like they're on fire!"

"That seems like a real hazard for a paper

thief," Donnie observed.

The big guy punched his palm, looking eager for a fight. "You!" he growled. "I'm going to grind your bones with my fists!"

"Oh, that's inspired," the smaller ninja said to the big guy, impressed. His voice was really raspy and creepy. Then he turned and pointed at us. "We're BOTH going to grind your bones."

"Riiiight," Raph drawled, unimpressed with these threats. "Listen, bubs, before we put OUR footprints on your faces, we gotta ask—what's with all the paper?"

The raspy-voiced ninja grabbed a sheet of paper and quickly folded it into a small origami warrior.

"Yay!" Mikey cheered. "Arts and crafts!"

But then the ninja threw the origami warrior at us. *BOOM!* There was a small explosion. From the smoke emerged . . .

. . . A FULL-SIZED NINJA WARRIOR, READY TO ATTACK!

"WHOOOAAA!" we all shouted, amazed.

The warrior had strange, glowing blue eyes that seemed to goggle around in his head. This thing was not human. The origami ninja ran up and knocked Raph across the room into the wall with one punch. *WHAM!*

"Uh, hey, maybe we should fight now and register our amazement later," Donnie suggested.

I was already moving toward the origami ninja.

ZWING! I swung my *odachi* sword, slicing right through him.

POOF! He exploded into pieces, which fluttered down all over us.

We were grossed out, but then I realized what it was. "Wait a minute. It's just confetti!"

"Oh, yeah," the others said, not grossed out anymore.

The raspy-voiced ninja made more origami warriors and flung them at us.

Raph swung his *tonfas*. Mikey whipped his *kusari-fundo*, knocking a couple into confetti with one blow.

But they just kept coming!

"We're getting nowhere fighting these guys," I said. "We gotta take out the source!"

CHAPTER SIX

I flipped off the paper stack and ran toward the small guy, but the big ninja blocked my way. I threw my best kicks and punches at him, but he blocked them all. "Think you're pretty good, huh?" I said.

"Indeed," he answered. He did a spinning back kick that sent me flying across the room and into a wall. *WHAM!*

I groaned. "You are good."

At that very moment, the small ninja

raised his arms. A strange energy filled the air. Wind started to blow like a storm was forming in the alley. All the stolen paper began to spin. It went faster and faster and grew higher and higher. Suddenly, there was a massive tornado of paper spinning before us. And it formed into . . .

. . . A GIANT NINJA WARRIOR!

It flexed its tremendous arms and growled a terrible growl, like a wild beast.

We stared, slack-jawed.

The huge warrior reached down and grabbed me in one gigantic hand, squeezing until I thought I'd burst!

Raph turned to Mikey and Donnie. "Any ideas?"

"It's piñata time!" Donnie said.

The three of them charged the giant ninja.

BOOM! BOOM! BOOM! BOOM!

Donnie and Mikey grabbed on to the fist he was holding me with, but then the gigantic ninja captured them with his other hand.

"Okay," Donnie gasped. "Does anyone have any other ideas? Because this isn't it!"

Raph spotted the smaller ninja punching his fists into each other. The giant ninja did the same thing, slamming me into Donnie and Mikey! The raspy-voiced guy was controlling the giant! Raph realized he had to take out the smaller ninja. "Hero Town!" he roared. "Population: ME!"

He sprinted between the giant origami ninja's feet, charging up his *tonfa* sticks with mystic power as he ran! A red glow surrounded Raph with power. When he reached the two original ninjas, he seized them with the *tonfas* and flipped them into a wall just like Lou Jitsu!

"HOT SOUP!" he yelled.

Raph stared at his *tonfas,* amazed at what he'd just done.

The giant origami ninja dropped me, Donnie, and Mikey, and collapsed into confetti! Shredded paper filled the cargo hold like snow.

Donnie, Mikey, and I popped up out of the confetti. But so did the two ninjas! They immediately started folding more origami warriors!

I pointed up at the ceiling. "Mikey! The sprinklers!"

"I'm on it!" Mikey yelled. He whipped his flaming *kusari-fundo* up at a sprinkler head. *WHOOSH!*

Water rained down, soaking all the paper. When the ninjas tried to make new origami warriors, they collapsed into mush. The smaller ninja tried folding one last warrior out of salami, but that soldier wobbled and collapsed, too.

"Eww!" Mikey said. "That's nightmare fuel, man!"

"Okay," Donnie observed. "Salami origami doesn't work."

Raph pointed to where the two ninjas had been seconds before. "Hey, look! They vanished!"

With the fight over, Raph noticed the pile of salami on the ground and reached for it. "NO, NO!" we cried.

He popped a slice in his mouth and chewed. Donnie, Mikey, and I were majorly grossed out.

"What?" Raph asked. "Five-second rule!"

Then Mikey asked, "So, does this count as a win?"

I put my arm around his shoulders. "Well, I dunno. Let's think about it. Did the bad guys get their big supply of paper? Uh, no. Did they build their army of soldiers? No. No, they didn't. Are they otherwise thwarted, and we unscathed?"

"Yes!" my three brothers answered together, smiling.

"Hero mission accomplished, my friends!" I said, grinning.

We high-fived and shouted, "HOT SOUP!"

WAR AND PIZZA

CHAPTER ONE

This is April. I'm going to tell you about the time the Turtles "helped" me at one of my many after-school jobs. It's unbelievable what a teenager has to go through to make even pitifully small amounts of money in New York City.

I was working at Albearto's Pizzera—this place where kids go to eat pizza, play games, and watch rusty old robots play instruments and sing songs. These robots are really kooky. They look like clunky animals and tomatoes and sticks of pepperoni. Albearto's is a popular spot for birthdays, and there was one going on at that moment. Actually, it was going out of control.

Kids were running around, screaming, diving into the ball pit—one kid had even gotten trapped in one of those glass boxes where you use a claw to grab a stuffed animal prize.

"How did you even get in there?" I asked, trying to lift the kid out with the claw.

"Whee!" was his only response. Even if he'd tried to explain how he got in there, I don't think he would have made any sense.

After two or three fumbling attempts, I was finally able to hoist him out of the stuffed animals. "Whee!" the kid said.

My manager walked up, shaking his head. "I hope we aren't headed for another of your epic party fails, Party Captain O'Neil."

I dropped the kid, jumped in front of the game to hide him, and smiled a big, confident fake smile.

"No way, sir! Tonight's the night I'm FINALLY getting a party all the way through Albearto's 'Happy Birthday' song and cake!"

"You better," the manager said. "This is your last chance." He stomped off.

"You got this, Party Captain O'Neil!" I told myself. The kid in the game gave me a thumbs-up. There was no time to fish him out now. I'd deal with him later.

I jumped onto the stage to introduce the singing robots, doing my best to get the kids excited.

"Get hyped, kids! He's coming to the stage to sing 'Happy Birthday,' so give a big

'What uuup' to the Cheese-Master of Bear-emonies, Albearto! With his Fun Time Band—Cheery Tomato and President Pepperoni!"

Dusty curtains slowly opened, revealing the old robots onstage. Albearto was, of course, a bear dressed in a chef's hat. Cheery Tomato held a guitar, while President Pepperoni was on drums.

"*Buongiorno*, kiddies!" Albearto said in his goofy voice, his mouth opening and closing in a way that didn't match his words at all. "I hear someone's a year older today, and I'm not just talking about my underwear!"

President Pepperoni hit the drums. *BA-DUM BUM!*

The kids just stared. One nine-year-old girl gave a small laugh, like she felt sorry for Albearto.

"Okay!" Albearto said. "Sing with me, kiddies! *Hap*—"

"Hey, Albearto!" the birthday boy shouted. "INCOMING!" He flung a pitcher of soda right at Albearto!

"NOOOOO!" I cried.

SPLOOSH! The soda hit him right in the mouth! Albearto sparked, smoked, and then broke down completely, slumping over.

"Boooooo," the nine-year-old girl yelled.

"This is the WORST!" the birthday boy shouted, even though it was totally his fault.

Realizing the show was over, the kids started running wild, dashing around the pizzeria and throwing anything they could get their hands on. It was like a riot!

"Not good," I said to myself. "Not good."

I whipped out my phone and punched in a familiar number.

In the Turtles' lair, Donnie answered his wrist com. "You're conversing with

Donatello."

"Dude, I need your help!" I pleaded. I explained how I needed him to fix Albearto. He said he and his brothers would be right over.

"Actually, I only need you, Donnie," I said. But he'd already hung up.

CHAPTER TWO

The four brothers burst into the backstage area through a rear door.

"Fixers in the house!" Raph said. "Swoopin' in to save the day!"

"That was fast!" I said. "Actually, I just needed Donnie—"

"Oh, we know," Raph said. "We just came for the free pizza." He turned to Mikey and Leo. "Remember, blend in like we're birthday robots."

"Aye aye, Captain," Mikey said in his best robot voice.

"Meep moop," Leo said. *"Meep moop."*

Raph, Mikey, and Leo stiffly walked toward the kitchen like robots. I hoped my boss wouldn't see them.

"So, Donnie," I said. "Hopefully this'll be a quick fix?"

But Donnie had already completely disassembled Albearto, with pieces spread all over the floor.

"Or a total teardown," I said, trying to stay positive. "That works."

CHAPTER THREE

I peeked through the curtain. The kids were still going crazy, running around like wild animals. Backstage, Donnie worked on Albearto with his battle shell's spider arm. "Short-circuiting conquered," he said. "Now to juice up his—"

"That's enough!" I told him, eager to get through the song and the cake. "I just need him to sing 'Happy Birthday.' And quiet the kids down so I don't get fired."

"Sure, he could just sing it," Donnie said, "or he could DAZZLE!"

"Please, please, no dazzling," I begged.

I couldn't believe it, but when I looked at Donnie, he was actually GETTING A LITTLE TEARY as he thought about how great he was going to make Albearto. Still working on the robot, Donnie said, "He might end up being the greatest entertainer-bot of his generation!"

"Please, Donnie," I begged. "Albearto doesn't need to—"

"Voilà!" Donnie said, as he finished reassembling the robot bear. "Albearto 2.14.2." When I looked confused, he explained, "I upgraded my upgrade in the middle of the upgrade."

I had to admit, Albearto looked fixed. Donnie pushed a button on Albearto's remote control. "Now to sync him to my remote," Donnie said. "And . . . it's showtime!"

The robot powered back up. "*Buongiorno,* kiddies!"

"Yeah!" I said. "Now let's go give Timmy the Albeartoiest birthday ever!" I peeked through the curtain. It was still chaos out there. "Ready?" I asked Donnie.

"Yep," he said, pressing a button on his remote.

I opened the curtain to reveal the new, improved Albearto. He had an electric guitar and flashy sunglasses. "*Buongiorno,* kiddies!" he said.

"Is he going to break again?" the nine-year-old girl asked. Timmy, the birthday boy, folded his arms across his chest and scowled.

"Hold on to your birthday hats, kiddies!" Albearto cried as he began to rock out on the electric guitar.

"And now for a little guitar solo," Donnie said, working the remote control. "You're welcome."

Albearto's solo was awesome! "Check me out!" he said. "I'm shredding this guitar like it's mozzarella!" The kids loved it!

I threw my fists in the air in triumph. "Looking good, D!" I told Donnie.

But then, as Albearto danced across the stage playing his guitar, the music started to skip and repeat. "Uh, hold on," Donnie said, trying to adjust the remote. "No. No, no, no! He should not be glitching. He should be rocking and/or rolling!"

A red light flashed on Donnie's remote, indicating that the battery was about to die. "Oh no!" he cried. "The battery! I knew I forgot to charge something!" The remote went dead. Donnie looked up at Albearto, who was leaping wildly around the stage.

"I can't stop him!"

Albearto started to swing the guitar around by its strap. But the guitar hit a stage light, breaking the bulb. *SMASH!* The neck of the guitar jammed into the light socket! *ZZAP!* Electricity surged through the guitar, blasting Albearto!

And then the lights went out.

CHAPTER FOUR

In the kitchen, Raph, Leo, and Mikey stopped chowing down on pizza when the lights went out. "This can't be good," Raph said.

Desperately trying to save the birthday party, I announced (in total darkness), "Okay. So that happened. But we can still sing 'Happy Birthday' without Albearto. *Happy birthday to–*"

Two glowing eyes lit up in the dark! The

lights came back on, and Albearto was moving! "Hey diddly ho, kiddies!" he said in a creepy voice. "Time to pump this party up! Let's play!"

As he staggered toward the kids, they all screamed and ran off.

"Donnie, can you, um . . . ?" I asked. What was he DOING?

Donnie desperately fumbled with the remote control. "I can fix this. I can fix this. I can totally fix this!" He banged his head against the remote. It fell to the floor and shattered. "You know what? Turns out I can't fix this."

Laughing a goofy, scary laugh, Albearto stomped toward Timmy with his arms stretched out toward him.

WHAM! I nailed the creepy robot with a metal pizza tray!

"Play nice, Albearto," I said.

The fake fur flew off his paws, revealing robotic claws underneath. Albearto's eyes sparked!

"Run, kid!" I told the birthday boy, pointing to the exit. He took off!

ZING! Albearto flexed his sharp metal claws, chuckling maniacally. "Thanks for the claws, April!"

"It knows my name?!" I said, blocking him with the tray.

"Claws are WAY better to open presents with!" Albearto said as he shredded the presents to bits.

I spotted some terrified kids still cowering under a table. "Who wants to play a fun game?" I asked in my cheeriest voice. "It's called Follow the Leader to Safety!"

I led the screaming kids to the exit, quickly telling them, "And tell your friends to celebrate at Albearto's after you're done fleeing for your lives!" When the last kid was out, I slammed the door closed, and turned to face . . .

. . . ALBEARTO! He was looming over me, laughing an insane laugh and lifting his sharp claws!

BAM! Raph flew in and punched Albearto away, shouting, "KNUCKLE SANDWICH!" Albearto crashed to the floor but stood right back up.

Wielding his *tonfa* sticks, Raph faced off against the rogue robot. "We'll fix it, April," he assured me. "He may have the crazy, but we got the numbers. Go ahead and bounce if you need to."

His eyes sparking, Albearto suddenly shot wires out of his mouth. Crackling with power, they attached to Cheery Tomato and President Pepperoni. Electricity surged through them, and they joined Albearto, staring at us aggressively.

"Uh, he's bringing the robots to life," Donnie said.

"No sweat," Raph said confidently. "Still got this."

Turning his head 180 degrees, Albearto shot out more wires, bringing dozens of little robotic moles from the Fun Time Mole Choir to life! They joined Albearto's evil robot army.

"Um," Raph said nervously, "you didn't have plans right now, did ya, April?"

CHAPTER FIVE

"Oh, I'm staying," I declared. "I'm Party Captain O'Neil, and I'm saving Timmy's party from disaster!" We heard a scream and turned to see Timmy surrounded by evil vole robots! "Right after I save Timmy," I added.

We leapt into action! While the Turtles battled Albearto, Cheery Tomato, and President Pepperoni, I scooped up Timmy. Then I grabbed the mallet from the Smack-

A-Vole game and said, "IT'S GO TIME!" As the robotic voles flew toward me, I batted them out of the air!

I didn't notice that three of the voles were sneaking up on me from the holes in the game. Then ... *WHACK!* Timmy slammed the voles away with a mallet of his own!

"Oh yeah!" I cheered. "Nice job, birthday boy!"

Timmy laughed nervously.

But the little voles weren't through. Together they lifted a rocket ride into the air and threw it at us! We dove out of the way, sliding right into the claw game. When we bumped into it, a panel opened, and the trapped kid jumped out and threw his fists in the air.

"Yippee!" he cheered. "I'm free!"

I grabbed him and tossed him right back in the glass box, along with Timmy. "You'll be safer in there," I explained. "Plus, you'll have a new friend!"

President Pepperoni slammed Mikey into a game where you rolled wooden balls into holes to win tickets for prizes. The robot pointed at Mikey. "President Pepperoni wants YOU . . . for his punching bag!"

Mikey picked up a wooden ball and whipped it at President Pepperoni, but the robot batted the ball back with his pepperoni sticks. Mikey ducked, and the ball went right into a hole. Bells rang, lights flashed, and prize tickets shot out of a slot.

"All right!" Mikey cheered. "Making it rain!" He scooped up balls and rapidly flung them at the robot. President Pepperoni managed to bat the first couple away but then got hit. *WHAM!*

Mikey used his *kusari-fundo* to lasso the robot and yank him into the game. *CRASH!*

Prize tickets flew out!

"Four score and twenty more tickets!" Mikey cheered.

In the ball pit, Cheery Tomato was jumping up and down on Donnie, shouting, "WHEE!"

"Ow! You're so cute, but so mean," Donnie cried. "Why do I always go for your type?"

With his mechanical spider arms, he grabbed Cheery Tomato and shot electricity through her, frying her circuits. As she powered down and sank into the balls, she said, "This doesn't make Cheery cheery," her voice getting slow and deep. She sank out of sight, waving goodbye, until ... she exploded!

Donnie dove out of the ball pit just in time. "I'll never eat ketchup again," he groaned.

Meanwhile, Leo swung his *odachi* sword

at Albearto. "You'd think as a birthday bot," Leo observed, "you'd be a little more chill at a birthday party!"

Albearto swung a heavy baking sheet. *WHAM!* He knocked Leo right into the window of the manager's office. I hoped he wouldn't notice! Leo slid to the floor, moaning, "Ow!"

Raph tried to charge his *tonfas* with mystic power, but he didn't really know how to do it. "Power Smash Jitsu!" he repeated a couple of times, knocking them together. The *tonfas* gave little puffs of smoke but didn't glow. "Or not!" Raph said, abandoning that tactic. He charged toward Albearto, roaring, "YAAAAHHH!"

CHAPTER SIX

But Albearto spotted Raph rushing toward him. The rampaging robot grabbed Raph by the arm and threw him into Leo, who was still on the floor. *WHAM!*

"If I can't have a birthday party," Albearto growled, "NOBODY CAN!"

Twirling his *kusari-fundo,* Mikey flew toward Albearto, yelling, "COWABUNGA!" But Albearto knocked him right into his two brothers. "I'm gonna crack you open like a birthday piñata!" the robot vowed, advancing on the pile of Turtles.

Albearto loomed over Leo, Raph, and Mikey, giggling and gloating. "Your sorry skills make me snicker! You're no match for the King of Birthday Parties, that's for sure!"

When he heard that, Donnie got an idea! "There's only one way to get through to this guy," he said, looking around for what he needed.

Albearto was about to finish off the three Turtles, when he heard Donnie saying, "Hey, Albearto! You can't be the King of Birthday Parties without having one of your own!" When the robot turned, he saw Donnie offering him Timmy's birthday cake on a cart.

The robot raised his claws to the sky, growling. But then he stopped. "Wait," he said in his normal voice. "What? A birthday party? For ME?!"

"Yes!" Donnie said, nodding. "Today's the day you were born!" Quickly adding "Through a total accident that is clearly nobody's fault." He handed the birthday cake to Albearto.

"A birthday cakey-wakey?" the robot asked, delighted. "For meesie-weesie?"

Donnie smiled. "Not just a cake, my friend. We've also got a little song for ya!" He started to sing. *"Happy birthday to you."*

Albearto beamed with joy as he looked around the room. Raph, Leo, and Mikey joined in the singing.

Here was my chance to save the party! I leapt on Albearto and whacked that robot with my mallet until he collapsed facedown in the birthday cake, snuffing out the candles! *WHAM!*

The four brothers just stared at me.

"Sing with me, guys," I ordered. "I am FINISHING this party! *Happy birthday . . . "* I noticed the stunned Turtles weren't singing. "Finish the song!"

"*. . . dear squirt,*" Raph guessed.

"*. . . dear kid,*" Leo tried.

"*. . . dear Albearto?*" Mikey sang.

"*. . . dear Timmy,*" Donnie sang, getting it right.

"Happy birthday to you!" we all finished together.

All our fighting and slamming and hammering had weakened the building. The pizzeria started to shake and collapse! The Turtles skedaddled.

Inside the claw game, Timmy pumped his fists. "Best birthday ever!"

The manager ran out of his office and saw the destruction. "My restaurant!" he wailed, clutching his head.

I tried to cheer him up. "On the upside, I finally made it through the birthday song!"

"That tears it, O'Neil!" he screamed, pointing at me. "YOU'RE—"

"Fired," I said, dropping my Party Captain badge into his hands. "Yeah, I figured. You can mail my last paycheck. Peace."

I hurried out of there. But as I walked out the door, I thought I saw something sparking, just for a second. . . .

It was Albearto's eye!